Beverly Lewis

Beverly Lewis Books for Young Readers

PICTURE BOOKS

Annika's Secret Wish • *Cows in the House*
In Jesse's Shoes • *Just Like Mama*
What Is Heaven Like?

THE CUL-DE-SAC KIDS

The Double Dabble Surprise
The Chicken Pox Panic
The Crazy Christmas Angel Mystery
No Grown-ups Allowed
Frog Power
The Mystery of Case D. Luc
The Stinky Sneakers Mystery
Pickle Pizza
Mailbox Mania
The Mudhole Mystery
Fiddlesticks
The Crabby Cat Caper
Tarantula Toes
Green Gravy
Backyard Bandit Mystery
Tree House Trouble
The Creepy Sleep-Over
The Great TV Turn-Off
Piggy Party
The Granny Game
Mystery Mutt
Big Bad Beans
The Upside-Down Day
The Midnight Mystery

Katie and Jake and the Haircut Mistake

www.BeverlyLewis.com

THE CUL-DE-SAC KIDS

Green Gravy

Beverly Lewis

BETHANY HOUSE PUBLISHERS
MINNEAPOLIS, MINNESOTA 55438

Green Gravy
Copyright © 1997
Beverly Lewis

Cover illustration by Paul Turnbaugh
Text illustrations by Janet Huntington

Published by Bethany House Publishers
11400 Hampshire Avenue South
Bloomington, Minnesota 55438

Bethany House Publishers is a division of
Baker Publishing Group, Grand Rapids, Michigan.

Printed in the United States of America

ISBN-13:   978-1-55661-985-4
ISBN-10:   1-55661-985-5

Library of Congress Cataloging-in-Publication Data

Lewis, Beverly, 1949–
        Green gravy / by Beverly Lewis.
            p.   cm. — (The cul-de-sac kids)
        Summary: As Student of the Week, Carly makes a wish
that her classmates celebrate St. Patrick's Day by wearing
green and eating green food but not everyone in the class
agrees.
        ISBN 1-55661-985-5 (pbk.)
        [1. Behavior—Fiction. 2. Brothers and sisters—Fiction.
3. Schools—Fiction.] I. Title. II. Series: Lewis, Beverly,
1949–   Cul-de-sac kids.
PZ7.L584Gr   1997
[Fic]—dc21   97–21032
                                                 CIP
                                                  AC

To
Claire Badger,
a delightful young reader
who is full of great story ideas.
(Thanks for "friendly freckles"!)

THE CUL-DE-SAC KIDS

ONE

Carly Hunter's stomach did a flitter-flop.

She looked up from her school desk.

The teacher had just called her name. But Miss Hartman looked happy, not frowny.

"You're the Student of the Week!" she said to Carly.

"I am?" Carly couldn't believe her ears.

"Please come to the front of the room," Miss Hartman said.

Carly got up and walked toward the teacher's desk.

Dee Dee Winters, Carly's best friend, gave high-fives. "Three cheers for Carly Hunter!" she said.

The others joined in. "Three cheers," they chanted.

Carly smiled and turned to face her classmates.

The teacher pinned a button on her sweater. It said *Student of the Week*. The words *Blossom Hill School* were spelled out at the bottom.

Miss Hartman gave Carly a piece of paper. "Give this to your parents. They can help you gather information about your life," she said. "For your special day."

"Thank you," Carly replied.

Wow!

This was going to be fun.

During the school year, Carly had paid close attention. Other students had been given this honor. To get picked, you had to be a good citizen. An extra good one.

Yay!

Before she sat down, Miss Hartman explained some things. "As you know, the honored student makes a wish," she said. "It can be anything. Within reason, of course."

For a moment, Carly thought. She glanced across the room at Dee Dee. Her friend was making hand motions.

What was she trying to say?

Dee Dee was pointing toward the wall calendar.

Carly looked at the calendar. She saw a big, green cloverleaf. It was marking St. Patrick's Day. March 17.

Now Dee Dee pointed to her own shirt. It was green-and-white checked.

The teacher was waiting. "Are you ready to make your wish?" she asked.

"I'm not sure," replied Carly.

She glanced at Dee Dee again.

Then she noticed Jimmy, her adopted

Korean brother. He was leaning forward. His dark eyes were shining.

Carly could just imagine what he was thinking. *Wish for more recesses*, he might say.

But she stared at the calendar. She looked at the big, green clover. She thought about March 17.

There was plenty of Irish in her family. Mostly on her mother's side.

She looked around the room again.

Lots of kids were something else—not Irish. Dee Dee was one of them. She had dark skin and deep brown eyes. Her hair had natural curls. Lucky for Dee Dee.

And there was Carly's adopted brother. Jimmy had olive skin and straight, black hair. His eyes slanted up a little.

She took a breath and held it in.

Was her wish the right one?

Maybe not.

The teacher and the students were still waiting.

Carly decided to make a secret wish. It was a before-the-wish wish. A worrywart wish.

She wished that her *special* wish would be just right.

By now, Jimmy wiggled in his seat.

Dee Dee wrinkled her nose.

Other students were restless, too.

At last, Carly breathed all her air out. It was time.

The Student of the Week's wish was ready.

TWO

Carly said, "My wish is . . ."

She looked at the calendar again. Today was Monday. Her special day was going to land on St. Patrick's Day!

On Wednesday. Just two more days.

"I want everyone to wear green," she said. "Because I'm Irish."

The kids started to clap.

All but Jimmy.

Their clapping made Carly smile.

That's when the greatest idea popped into her head.

"Oh, one more thing," she said out loud.

The teacher looked surprised. "Only *one* wish."

Carly turned to her. "But this is lots like the other wish."

"Well, let's hear it." Miss Hartman leaned over so Carly could whisper in her ear.

"Everyone must eat green food for St. Patrick's Day," Carly whispered.

Miss Hartman stood up straight. She was smiling. "I don't see why we can't have this wish, too," she said. "It's a two-part wish. Part A and part B."

Then she told the class, "We'll all wear green clothes and eat green foods. Let's make Carly's wish come true."

Someone said, "Yucko."

It was Jimmy. His hand shot up.

"Yes?" the teacher said.

"Everyone do this?" Jimmy asked in broken English.

Miss Hartman nodded. "It's Carly's wish. And she's our Student of the Week."

Jimmy's cheeks sagged. "I not eat green food. I eat mashed potato and gravy." He held up the school menu. "I buy hot lunch on Carly Hunter day!" He shook his head and made a fuss face.

Carly felt her neck getting hot. *Jimmy is a Sour-Pie brother*, she thought.

She wanted to stamp her foot and holler. But she walked to her desk and sat down.

She felt Dee Dee's hand on her shoulder. Dee Dee's desk was right behind hers.

"Jimmy's mad," whispered Dee Dee.

Carly looked over her shoulder. "That's his problem," she said.

Then she looked at Jimmy but couldn't see his face. He'd put his head down on his desk.

"Now what?" Carly said softly, but mostly to herself.

17

Jimmy was pouting again. He'd just have to get over it.

Here in America, kids liked to have fun on special days. He'd have to start acting more American.

Like it or not!

★ ★ ★

It was after school.

Her mother waited at the front door. "How was your day?"

"I'm Student of the Week!" Carly exclaimed. "I have to tell the class all about me. About my life."

She showed the paper with directions from Miss Hartman.

Mother smiled a happy face. "Would you like to show the class some baby pictures?"

"Yes!" Carly said. "And what else?"

"How about a picture of Snow White, our dog?" said Mother.

"Good idea!" Carly was excited. "Can I

take Quacker, my duck, to school?"

Her mother laughed. "A duck at school? I don't know about that."

"But she's my pet," Carly said. "She's part of the family."

Carly went to look outside. The ducks, Quacker and Jack, were in their pen. They waddled through the dirt. They pecked at their feed.

"Well . . . maybe you're right," she said. "Maybe it's not a good idea for a duck to go to school."

Her mother studied the teacher's idea list. "What about your favorite foods?" she said.

"Sweets," said Carly. "I love sweets."

"Then we'll bake cookies for everyone," her mother said. She was checking off the list. "Can we fit everything into a shoe box?" she asked.

"We'll try," said Carly. "But not my duck."

Her mother agreed. "Definitely not."

"I know! I'll draw a picture of Quacker," Carly suggested. "We have art class tomorrow."

Her mother nodded. "I like that idea. Good thinking."

Carly leaned over her mother's shoulder. She looked at the list. "Anything else?"

"It would be nice to show pictures of your whole family," her mother said.

Carly thought about that. "OK with me," she said. "But none of Jimmy."

Her mother had a strange look. "Why not? He's your brother."

"But he's in my class," Carly said. "Everyone knows what Jimmy looks like."

He looks like a sour pie, she thought. *Because that's what he is!*

"Why don't you think about it," her mother said.

"I'll think," Carly said. But she wasn't so sure.

20

THREE

At supper, Jimmy poked at his food.
Carly watched.

"Sit up and eat, son," their father said.

"No like peas," Jimmy said. He pushed his plate away.

Carly shook her head. "He's still upset."

Mother perked up her ears. "Why is that?"

"Because of me," Carly said.

Abby, her big sister, frowned. "What did *you* do to him?"

Carly jerked her head and glared at

21

Abby. "I didn't do anything. He's mad because I got picked for Student of the Week."

"Good going for Carly!" Shawn said. He was Jimmy's Korean brother. His big brother.

Now Shawn was glaring at Jimmy. "Not good being mad at little sister," Shawn said. He began to talk in Korean.

Jimmy covered his ears with his hands. "Carly make class wear green," he whined. "She make us eat yucko green food."

Abby and Shawn were laughing.

So was their mother, but not very long.

Their father spoke up. "Wearing green might be fun."

"And just think of all the cool *green* foods there are," said Abby.

"Yeah, like celery," said Carly.

"And pears," Shawn said.

"Yucko," Jimmy said. His face was fussy.

"Spinach has a nice green color," said their father. He was smiling now.

"So does broccoli," said Mother.

"Lettuce is green," said Carly.

"Yuck, yuck . . . yucko," chanted Jimmy.

Their father frowned. "I want you to practice eating green foods. Starting right now, with your peas."

Jimmy shot eye darts at Carly. He muttered something in Korean.

Then he picked up his spoon. One by one, he shot the peas across the table. Right at Carly!

Mother's eyebrows popped up.

Father scooted his chair back. "Time out," he told Jimmy. "Let's have a talk in your bedroom."

Jimmy's face got all purple and red. Both colors at once. He said, "Excuse, please," and left the table.

"Whew! He's in big trouble," Carly whispered.

Her mother put a finger to her lips. "Jimmy must learn to behave," she explained.

"He's a sour pie," Carly said.

"Calling names won't help," Abby said.

Their mother agreed. "Let's be kind."

Carly nodded her head. Mother was always saying words like that. Good-citizen words.

"It's not easy to be nice all the time," said Carly.

"I understand," said Mother. "But it's good to keep trying."

Carly blinked her eyes. "You should've seen Jimmy pouting at school."

Mother patted her long curls.

"I wish Daddy would come to school on St. Patrick's Day," Carly muttered.

"What for?" Abby asked.

"To make Jimmy wear green," said Carly. "And so he'll eat a green lunch."

"Who cares about that?" Abby said.

"I care," said Carly. "It's *my* special day!"

"You should hear yourself," said Abby. "If Jimmy's a sour pie, what's that make you?"

"A sour SOMEBODY," answered Carly. She sat up straight. She wiped her mouth with a napkin.

"Girls, girls," their mother said.

Abby got up from the table and went to the sink.

Carly wondered what her sister was thinking. She probably thought Miss Hartman should change her mind. Maybe someone else should be Student of the Week. Someone not so sour!

"Am I a sweet girl?" Carly asked her mother.

"Most of the time," Mother replied.

Abby returned to the table. "Nobody's perfect," she said.

"You think *you* are," Carly whispered.

Abby frowned. "That's not true!"

"Oh, really?" Carly felt a fuss coming.

So did their mother. "All right, you two. Clean up the kitchen." She went to the living room.

Carly carried two dishes to the sink. She spied the water spray. She thought about spraying Abby.

When Abby wasn't looking, she picked up the sprayer.

She aimed.

"Better not," Shawn warned.

But Carly didn't listen.

Swoosh!

Water splashed on the back of Abby's head.

"Hey!" Abby shouted.

Carly dropped the sprayer and ran to her bedroom.

She closed the door and pushed against it. "I'm a sour Somebody," she whispered to herself.

She waited for Abby to pound on the door.

No sound came.

She counted to twenty-five.

Still nothing.

But soon her mother's voice came through the door. "I need your help in the kitchen, please."

Slowly, Carly opened the door.

There stood her mother. And drippy Abby.

"Somebody needs to say 'sorry,'" her mother said. "Then you may wipe up the kitchen floor."

Carly did a gulp.

She was NOT a good citizen. Not one bit.

FOUR

It was Tuesday afternoon.

Art class!

Carly loved art.

She liked to daydream before she made a picture.

Daydreaming was like night dreaming. Except not quite. It happened when you were awake. It was the best kind of dreaming. Because you could plan it.

Well, sorta.

Carly stared out the art room window. Staring was a big part of daydreaming.

That's when she got an idea.

It was a GREEN idea. Another one!

Tomorrow was her special day. It was also St. Patrick's Day.

"I'll make a Pinch Rule," she whispered.

Dee Dee tapped her on the arm. "Who are you talking to?"

"Myself."

"How come?" asked Dee Dee.

"I'll tell you at recess."

"Tell me now," Dee Dee insisted.

"OK," Carly said. She whispered in Dee Dee's ear.

"What?" Dee Dee asked. "I didn't hear you."

The art teacher was coming. Time to get to work.

"Tell ya later," said Carly.

She picked up her sketch pencil. She made a picture of Quacker, one of her pet ducks.

Then Carly stopped drawing and looked at the sketch.

Sker-runch! She wadded up the paper.

She tried again. Her duck looked like a too-fat bowling pin.

Ducks are too hard, she decided.

So she daydreamed. And stared a lot.

She thought about tomorrow. She thought about the Pinch Rule.

Sour-Pie Jimmy was sitting across the room.

She stared at him, too.

He didn't want to wear green tomorrow. He'd said so last night. He was going to spoil everything!

Now he was drawing something. He was working very hard.

When Jimmy looked up, she caught his eye.

Carly made a mad face. Capital M!

But Jimmy grinned back.

He held up his drawing. It was a clover leaf. A RED one.

Whoever heard of that?

Carly knew he was making fun of her green-day idea.

You'll be sorry, she thought.

The Pinch Rule was going to be great.

By afternoon recess, everyone would know about it.

Especially Sour-Pie Jimmy.

Boy, was he gonna get it tomorrow!

★ ★ ★

At recess, Carly and Dee Dee made a circle. A tiny, secret circle. Just for two best friends.

Carly told her friend about the Pinch Rule. "Whoever isn't wearing green gets pinched," she said. "That's the Pinch Rule."

"Isn't the whole class gonna wear green?" Dee Dee asked.

"Jimmy's not," Carly replied.

"Then he's the only one who's gonna get pinched," said Dee Dee. But she wasn't laughing.

"I know." Carly grabbed a swing.

Dee Dee took the one next to her. "So why do you wanna have a Pinch Rule?" she asked.

Carly didn't want to lie. That wouldn't be a good citizen.

"Is it 'cause of Jimmy?" Dee Dee asked.

"Jimmy's a sour pie. That's what!" Carly leaned back in her swing. She made it go high into the sky.

"I thought you liked Jimmy," Dee Dee shouted. "Ever since your parents adopted him, it's been you and him. Good friends."

Carly didn't say anything. She wished Dee Dee would keep quiet. Too many kids were standing around.

"Jimmy's your brother, remember?" Dee Dee said.

"I didn't say he wasn't," Carly hollered back.

Dee Dee dragged her feet and stopped

33

swinging. She got off. And she stood right where Carly could see her.

But Carly stared up at the sky. "Quit buggin' me," she said.

Dee Dee said, "Yes, Your Royal *Highness.*"

Then she walked away.

"Oh, great," Carly whispered. "The Student of the Week has another enemy."

She—Carly Hunter—wasn't so special. She knew it for sure.

So did her best friend.

And probably her brother.

She felt like crying.

FIVE

It was Carly's special day.

"Make Jimmy wear green!" Carly wailed.

Her mother shook her head. "I'm not going to force him," she said. "Jimmy's Korean, not Irish."

"But he *has* to," Carly told her. "The whole class is supposed to wear green and eat green."

"Well, I gave Jimmy some lunch money," her mother said. "So it's up to the school cook, I guess."

Carly wanted to stamp her foot. But

she knew better. Her mother would give her extra chores. For sure.

She went to her room. She made her bed and folded her pajamas. Cleaning up helped to take the "M" out of mad!

On top of that, she counted to fifty. Very slowly.

Soon she was drawing a picture of Quacker. *This* time she looked out the window at her duck. She took her time and did a good job.

The sketch turned out just ducky.

She pinned on her *Student of the Week* button.

Now she was ready to make her green lunch.

First, she washed two big pieces of celery.

No peanut butter today. Wrong color.

Next, she put two pieces of lettuce together. She added sliced dill pickles.

She found some raw broccoli. A little avocado dip would taste good.

She helped herself to a handful of Spanish olives.

Her green meal was done. All but the drink.

A can of lemon-lime pop was easy. Nice and green, too.

Before she left, she reached into the cookie jar.

Mm-m, yum!

She'd helped her mother bake beautiful green clover cookies. With ooey, gooey green topping.

"Take plenty for your friends," her mother said.

"Teacher too?" Carly asked.

"Help yourself." Her mother found a plastic bag.

Carly put a bunch of cookies inside. "Maybe *now* Jimmy will eat something green," she said.

Her mother smiled. "Maybe, but maybe not."

"Why's he so stubborn?" asked Carly.

"Stubborn?" her mother said. "You could be wrong about that, dear. Jimmy might be feeling something else."

"Like what?" Carly asked. She couldn't think of anything.

"Jimmy needs to be himself," her mother said. "He's still getting used to America. And to all of us." She kissed Carly good-bye. "Do you have your shoe box full of things?"

"In my room," Carly said. "I have everything I need for my special day."

Everything but a best friend and a nice little brother, she thought.

That added up to nothing much!

"Take good care of our family pictures," her mother reminded her.

"I will," Carly said. "I promise."

"I'll carry the cookies," Abby said.

"Thank you," Carly said.

She was trying hard to be a good citizen.

★ ★ ★

Carly stuck with her big sister, Abby. And her big brother, Shawn. They walked across the street together.

So did Stacy Henry, Abby's best friend. Eric Hagel, too.

They were four of the older Cul-de-sac Kids. The rest of the kids in the club were already at school.

Miss Hartman's outside door was easy to see.

Super easy!

It was the one with all the green kids. A ribbon of green stretched out across the playground.

Carly saw something else. Something purple.

It's Jimmy, she thought. *He's spoiling my day*.

"Make sure you don't drop your pictures," Abby said.

"Mommy already told me that," Carly shot back.

"Hey, what's the matter?" Abby said. "I

40

was only trying to help."

"Well, I don't need any help." Carly stamped off.

It was OK to stamp in the school yard. Abby couldn't stop her.

"Guess I'll just eat up your cookies!" called Abby.

Carly spun around. "No! No!"

Abby hurried over. "Here," she said. "I was only kidding."

"Don't be a sour pie like Jimmy," muttered Carly to herself. Carefully, she carried the cookie bag and the shoe box.

Now . . . where was Dee Dee?

Carly searched. The green student line was a problem. Everyone looked the same!

Finally, she found her friend. Dee Dee's natural curls had a big green bow.

Carly waved to her. But Dee Dee didn't wave back.

Neither did Jimmy. He was at the end of the line.

"You look nice and green," Carly said.

Dee Dee didn't smile. "So do you."

Something was strange about Dee Dee's voice. It sounded like a flat tire.

"What's the matter?" Carly asked.

"Nothin' much," Dee Dee said.

She always said that when she was upset.

Carly got in line behind her. But Dee Dee didn't turn around. She didn't even look at Carly's clover cookies!

What's her problem? she wondered.

Carly could hardly wait for the bell.

SIX

Miss Hartman was writing on the board.

Her suit was bright green. Her green-and-blue blouse was all swirly.

When everyone was seated, she called the roll.

Jimmy was the only one missing.

"Is your brother sick?" Miss Hartman asked Carly.

Carly turned around. She looked all around the room. "I just saw him at the end of the line," she said.

Dee Dee tapped her on the shoulder.

"Look out the window. Jimmy's hiding. "

Carly stretched up, up out of her seat.

Her brother was sitting on the slide.

"There he is!" Carly pointed.

"Oh, dear," Miss Hartman said and rushed out the door.

Everyone jumped up to see.

Carly and Dee Dee got out of their seats, too.

"What's going on?" Dee Dee asked Carly.

"Who knows."

"Looks like Jimmy's got some markers," one girl called.

Everyone rushed to the window. They crowded in.

Carly was too short. She couldn't see.

Dee Dee crawled up on someone's desk. She started to giggle.

"What's funny?" Carly asked.

"Jimmy's painting dots on his nose," Dee Dee said.

"Dots? What for?" Carly asked.

44

"How would I know?" Dee Dee said.

The kids watched for a moment.

"Here comes the teacher!" someone said. "And Jimmy!"

They darted to their seats. Like scared mice.

Miss Hartman came inside, grinning. Silently, she guided Jimmy to his seat.

Carly stared. She wasn't daydreaming. Not at all.

Now everyone was staring.

Dee Dee was right. Jimmy *did* have dots on his nose.

But they weren't just any kind of dots.

They were GREEN ones!

"Those are some strange freckles," one boy joked.

Jimmy spoke up. "Friendly freckles." He laughed.

Miss Hartman sat at her desk. "Quiet, class," she said.

Everyone settled down.

"Every student in this class has helped

45

make Carly's wish come true," Miss Hart-man said. "Happy St. Patrick's Day."

The kids chattered a bit. They were saying "Happy St. Patrick's Day" to each other.

But Carly wasn't. She was staring at Jimmy.

His friendly green freckles went all across his nose. They spilled over onto his cheeks.

Carly was no dummy. She could see right through those Sour-Pie freckles.

Jimmy had tricked her. On purpose!

He'd tricked her with those green freckles.

She couldn't use the Pinch Rule on him.

It was no good now.

Rats!

SEVEN

It was time for morning recess.

Miss Hartman's class flew out the side door.

"Jimmy's a smart one," Dee Dee said. "He's wearing green, after all."

"Whose side are you on?" asked Carly.

Dee Dee didn't say anything. She rubbed her ear.

Carly stared at her.

"Not nice to stare," Dee Dee said.

"I wanna know whose side you're on," Carly said.

Dee Dee sniffed. But she didn't talk.

"Aw, c'mon," Carly pleaded. "Talk to me."

Dee Dee shook her head. "Only if you fix things up."

"With who?" Carly asked.

"You know who," Dee Dee said. "Start treatin' your brother nicer!"

Carly felt a fuss face coming. "You can't tell me what to do, Dee Dee Winters!"

She dashed to the swings.

Dee Dee ran the opposite way. She went in Miss Hartman's classroom door.

"You're a squealer," Carly said out loud. She stamped her foot.

"Who's tattling?"

Carly turned her head.

There stood Abby and Stacy.

"Are you fussing with Dee Dee?" Abby said.

Carly pouted. "Nobody's business."

Abby sat on the swing next to her. "You look pretty today," she said. "I like your green polka-dot skirt."

Carly shook her head. "I know what you're doing," she said. "I'm no dummy."

"Didn't say you were," Abby told her.

"So why are you saying I look pretty?" Carly asked.

"Listen to me," her big sister said. "You're the Student of the Week, right?"

Carly nodded. She bit her lower lip. "Guess you don't think I oughta be."

Stacy stepped up. She leaned too close to Carly's face. "Abby didn't mean that. You're a good citizen, Carly."

"Just not a *perfect* citizen," said Carly.

Abby scratched her head. "Don't say that."

Stacy glanced at Abby and lifted her shoulders. "Here comes someone," she said.

Carly looked up. Dee Dee was coming toward them.

"Hey, look, she's smiling," Abby said.

"It's a Sour-Pie smile," said Carly. "I know a squealer when I see one!"

EIGHT

The bell rang. Morning recess was over.

Carly hurried inside the classroom. She looked at Miss Hartman's face.

Is she upset? Carly wondered.

She couldn't tell. Not for sure.

Carly turned around in her seat. "Why did you squeal?" she asked Dee Dee.

"I just said what *you* said," Dee Dee replied. "And Miss Hartman said that it wasn't very nice."

Carly muttered, "Especially for a good citizen."

"What?" Dee Dee said.

"Oh, nothing," replied Carly. She wanted to cry.

Nothing was turning out right. Nothing at all.

Jimmy was getting away with wearing purple.

Dee Dee was mad. Capital M!

Miss Hartman was taking sides.

And . . . oh no!

She was putting "good-citizen" stars beside Jimmy's name. Up on the board where everyone could see.

Why? she wondered. *Jimmy doesn't deserve stars!*

She felt Dee Dee tapping her back. "Look. Jimmy's earning points," Dee Dee said.

Carly didn't turn around.

How could Miss Hartman do this?

Dee Dee kept whispering, "Jimmy didn't wanna wear green, remember? He's not Irish one bit! But he followed your wish, Carly. He wore green. Now *that's* a good citizen."

"Shh!" said Miss Hartman. "It's time for our Student of the Week. Carly Hunter, will you please come forward?"

Carly was upset. She twisted the eraser off her pencil.

Ka-pop!

It sailed over Dee Dee's desk and landed on Jimmy's head.

"What was that?" asked the teacher.

Jimmy felt the top of his head. He found the round pink ball. "Eraser drop down from sky," he said.

The kids laughed.

Carly froze. Now what?

Miss Hartman went around the room. She looked at everyone's pencil.

She came to Carly's desk and looked at her pencil.

The pink top was missing.

Carly looked down. "I didn't mean to," she said. "It was a mistake."

Dee Dee giggled behind her. "That's what erasers are for—mistakes!"

Everyone was laughing even harder.

Suddenly, Carly felt sick. "Excuse me," she said.

Off she ran to the girls' room.

★　★　★

First thing, Carly turned on the water. Cold water.

She slapped some on her face.

Then she dried off with a paper towel.

The face in the mirror was a fuss face. Capital F!

"What's the matter with me?" she said out loud.

Soon Miss Hartman came in. "Are you all right?"

Carly shook her head. "I don't know."

"Maybe the nurse should check you," said her teacher.

Miss Hartman took her to the little

square room. It smelled like mushroom soup.

The nurse had her sit down. She checked for a fever. She made her say "AHHHH!"

"You seem normal," the nurse said. "Maybe a little rest will help."

"OK. I'll rest," Carly said. She went to the cot to lie down.

But rest was impossible. Things were on her mind. Things like green foods and lunchtime. And Jimmy's not-green hot lunch.

She thought about the Pinch Rule. It was *Ker-plooey.*

Why not a Lunch Rule, too? A rule for anyone who didn't eat green foods.

Like Sour-Pie Jimmy!

She looked at the clock. It wouldn't be long now until lunch.

Would her brother trick her again?

NINE

Carly stared at the wall in the nurse's room.

She let herself daydream.

Jimmy was wearing a sour apple pie. It was smashed on his head. It had rotten green apples in it. And long green worms.

Carly shivered. She took a breath.

"How are you feeling?" asked the nurse.

"I need a drink of water, please," Carly said.

The nurse helped her up.

"Thank you," said Carly.

The lady in white let the water run. She gave her the full glass.

"Is it time for lunch yet?" Carly asked.

"Almost," said the nurse. "Are you hungry?"

Carly nodded and scooted off the cot. "I think I'm better now."

The nurse walked her back to Miss Hartman's room. "Tell your teacher if you're sick again."

"Thank you very much," Carly answered.

The nurse smiled. "What a polite girl."

"Thank you." Carly smiled, too.

The nurse was right. She *was* polite. Most of the time.

Carly opened the classroom door.

Miss Hartman was checking hand-writing papers.

Quickly, Carly went to her seat and took out her notebook.

"We're making *P*'s and *D*'s today," Miss Hartman told her. "For St. Patrick's Day."

Carly made her letters curly.

"That's not right," Dee Dee said in her ear.

But Carly didn't turn around. She made seven more letters. Each more curly than the other.

When Jimmy wasn't looking, Carly stared at him. She could see his paper. He was drawing a clover leaf at the top.

A green one!

Would he eat a green lunch, too?

★   ★   ★

At last it was lunchtime.

Miss Hartman's green students walked to the cafeteria.

Carly watched Jimmy. She didn't let him out of sight.

"Feeling better?" asked Dee Dee. She didn't wait for Carly to answer. "Still mad at your brother?"

"Not nice to be nosy," answered Carly.

She headed to a different table. Abby

58

and Stacy were sitting there. Jason Birchall and Dunkum Mitchell were there, too. And Shawn, of course.

"Hi, Carly," they all said.

"Can I sit here?" she asked.

"Well, I don't know if you *can*, but you may," Stacy said.

Carly smiled. Stacy liked to correct the way kids talked. She had the best speech in the cul-de-sac.

"Why aren't you sitting with your class?" Abby asked.

Carly lifted one shoulder. "Don't wanna."

She kept looking over at Jimmy. He was in the hot-lunch line now. And it looked like his friendly freckles were gone.

Carly thought about the Lunch Rule. "Is there any green food for hot lunch?" she asked.

Stacy laughed. "Our cook's not *that* creative."

59

"Well, I am!" Jason Birchall said. He held up a long, skinny tube. "This is my dessert."

Jason didn't just like the color green, he loved it. Especially green things like bullfrogs. Dill pickles, too.

Carly looked at the long tube. "What's it for?" she asked.

"It's cake icing," Jason said. "Wanna squeeze?"

"Maybe later," Carly said.

She stared at Jason's lunch. It was definitely a St. Patrick's Day meal. There were bunches of green grapes, slices of green melon, and a cup of green Jell-O. And a giant dill pickle.

"Hey, you're eating all green foods," she said.

"Green as a bean!" Jason chanted. He poked his pointer fingers in the air and jerked his head around.

The kids at the table laughed. So did Carly.

"Green as a bean!" they joined in.

Kids were looking at them. Mostly Miss Hartman's class, on the other side of the cafeteria.

Carly didn't mind.

She opened her sack lunch. She stopped long enough to glance across at her younger brother.

Jimmy had just set his lunch tray down.

Carly could see his plate. There was brown meat and gravy and some white mashed potatoes. The other vegetable was orange. Carrots!

Nice colors, but the wrong ones!

Stacy was right. The school cook wasn't very creative. Or maybe she wasn't Irish.

"There isn't a scrap of hot green food anywhere!" Carly said.

Stacy and Abby nodded. "That's true," said Stacy.

"Isn't anybody else remembering St.

Patrick's Day?" Carly asked.

Abby teased, "Looks like part B of your wish isn't working."

"Hey!" Carly turned to her sister. "Do ya have to tell the whole world?"

Abby just smiled. "It's kinda cute, that's all."

"Not *cute*," Carly said. "Cute's for babies." And she slid off her seat.

"Hey, don't forget your green lunch," Abby called.

"Forget you!" Carly snapped.

She picked up her lunch sack. Then she marched to the other side of the cafeteria.

TEN

Carly went to Jimmy's table and sat down. She glanced around at the lunches.

Everyone in her class was having green stuff for lunch. There was split pea soup and lots of celery sticks. One girl even had some raw spinach!

No one at their table was having hot lunch.

No one except Jimmy.

He didn't seem to care about her wish. Part A or part B. Nope. He sprinkled some salt and pepper on his gravy. And he dug right in.

"How's it taste?" Carly asked him.

"Very good." It sounded like *velly* good.

Carly stared at his tray. "Nothing's green on your plate," she whined.

Jimmy nodded. "I not eat green. I NOT Irish."

"Where are your friendly freckles?" she asked.

"Not like green dot face," he said.

The boy next to Jimmy laughed.

Jimmy joined in.

That did it!

Carly leaped up. She flew across the cafeteria to Abby's table.

Jason's tube of cake icing was in plain view.

"Mind if I squeeze this?" she asked.

Jason didn't have a chance to answer. She was gone before he could say "St. Patrick's Day."

At Jimmy's table, Carly hid the icing behind her. She hurried around to Jimmy. "I get my wish!" she said.

She leaned over Jimmy's shoulder.

And . . .

Squeeeeeeze!

Out came the gooey, green icing.

Plop!

It landed in Jimmy's gravy.

"Eew!" The kids at the table groaned.

"Happy St. Patrick's Day!" she sing-sang to her brother.

Jimmy's eyes were big now. Not angry, just big.

Slowly, he picked up his fork and took a bite.

The kids watched. They leaned toward him.

Dee Dee moved over to their table. She wanted to see what was going on.

"How's it taste *now*?" teased Carly.

"Green gravy not bad," Jimmy said.

He took another bite.

Dee Dee said, "I can't believe he's eating it."

"Green gravy good stuff," Jimmy said.

"I not Irish, but I eat green gravy!"

Miss Hartman's kids chanted, "Green gravy . . . green gravy . . ."

Across the cafeteria, Abby and her friends were staring.

Carly didn't mind.

She went around and squeezed green icing on pickles, Jell-O, and spinach. She squeezed it on lettuce and green pears.

It was a "double dabble" lunchtime. That's exactly what Abby would say.

Jason Birchall came running over. "Hey, don't use it all," he hollered.

"Thanks for the big squeeze," Carly said. She gave him the smashed-up tube. "You made my green wish come true."

Jason jigged around and acted silly. Then he trailed a string of icing onto his tongue.

Now *all* the kids were looking at Jason.

The lunchroom teacher blew a whistle.

Yikes. Carly hurried to sit down.

"Quiet!" the teacher called.

Everyone tried to settle down. It wasn't easy.

The kids at Jimmy's table were holding in the giggles.

The kids at Abby's table were tasting Jason's icing.

Carly was having too much fun.

She forgot all about the Lunch Rule.

ELEVEN

Carly carried her shoe box to Miss Hartman's desk.

She set down her bag of green cookies.

The teacher said, "There are fifteen stars beside Carly's name. She has earned the good citizenship award."

Carly took a deep breath. She hoped she hadn't let her teacher down. Or her classmates.

"Everyone listen carefully," said Miss Hartman. She nodded for Carly to begin.

"My name is Carly Anne Hunter," Carly said. "My middle name is *always* spelled with an 'e' on the end. I was born seven years ago. And I'm Irish on my mother's side."

She showed a picture of a fluffy white puppy. "This is Snow White. She's the color of clean snow."

Next, Carly held up a drawing of her duck. "This is Quacker," she said. "Her brother's name is Jack. Quacker and Jack are brother and sister."

The girls giggled.

The boys tried not to.

Someone asked, "Do your ducks fight?"

Carly nodded her head. "Like cats and dogs," she said.

She was ready to talk about her favorite foods. "I like sweets best." The clover cookies got passed around.

She noticed that Jimmy took two.

At last, she showed her family picture. "This is the whole Hunter family," she said.

She pointed to each person, starting

with her parents. "My father's English and my mother's Irish. But they learned to like Korean food in four months."

Next she pointed to Abby. "This is my big sister. She's the president of the Cul-de-sac Kids. It's a club. Abby makes up words like 'double dabble.' "

Carly pointed to a tall, skinny boy. "Shawn's nine years old. He plays soccer and the violin. His Korean name is Li Sung Jin, and he's my adopted big brother. Snow White is really *his* pet."

She picked up the dog's picture again.

Miss Hartman asked a question. "Is Snow White a Shih Tzu dog?"

"Yes," Carly answered. "Her doggie family tree goes back to ancient China."

"Do you know what Shih Tzu means?" asked the teacher.

"My father told me," Carly said. "It means *Lion Dog*. These pets were watch-dogs in the Chinese royal courts."

"Wow," someone whispered.

"Cool," someone else said.

Carly spoke up. "But better than all that is someone in this class. Someone very special." She pointed to Jimmy and asked him to stand up.

"You all know Jimmy. He's my adopted brother. He's Shawn's birth brother."

Jimmy was smiling.

"Will you come stand with me?" she asked him.

Her brother nodded. "I come."

Carly smiled at Jimmy. "Here is the best citizen I know," she said. "And a good sport."

She told about the green gravy. For Miss Hartman's sake.

Then she turned to Jimmy. "I'm sorry for being selfish. A good citizen is NOT selfish."

She took off her *Student of the Week* pin.

She put it on Jimmy.

Miss Hartman was smiling the biggest smile.

Everyone else was clapping.

Except Jimmy.

He pulled out his marker and stood on tippy-toes.

"What are you gonna do?" Carly asked.

"I draw green Irish heart on sister face," he said. "Happy Carly Day!"

Carly felt like crying.

Happy, happy tears. Capital H!

And she never ever said Sour-Pie Jimmy again.

THE CUL-DE-SAC KIDS SERIES
Don't miss #15!
BACKYARD BANDIT MYSTERY

Stacy Henry wants to earn extra money for the Cul-de-sac Kids club. But she can't get permission from Abby, the club president, who is out of town.

The rest of the kids vote to go ahead with the yard sale. But some of their treasures disappear one night.

Is there a bandit in the neighborhood?

Who is stealing from the Cul-de-sac Kids? And why?

ABOUT THE AUTHOR

Beverly Lewis is part Irish, but only a wee bit. The idea for this story came from her children, Julie, Janie, and Jonathan. Each of them received the honor of Student of the Week during grade school.

Now they are teenagers and help create cover ideas for the Cul-de-sac Kids books.

Beverly likes her mashed potatoes with *brown* gravy. (Capital B!) She tried eating cake icing on top, and it made her write this funny book.

If you like humor and mystery, watch for more Cul-de-sac Kids books. You just might discover a new food group!

Also by Beverly Lewis

The Beverly Lewis Amish Heritage Cookbook

GIRLS ONLY (GO!)
Youth Fiction

Dreams on Ice	*Follow the Dream*
Only the Best	*Better Than Best*
A Perfect Match	*Photo Perfect*
Reach for the Stars	*Star Status*

SUMMERHILL SECRETS
Youth Fiction

Whispers Down the Lane	*House of Secrets*
Secret in the Willows	*Echoes in the Wind*
Catch a Falling Star	*Hide Behind the Moon*
Night of the Fireflies	*Windows on the Hill*
A Cry in the Dark	*Shadows Beyond the Gate*

HOLLY'S HEART
Youth Fiction

Best Friend, Worst Enemy	*Straight-A Teacher*
Secret Summer Dreams	*No Guys Pact*
Sealed With a Kiss	*Little White Lies*
The Trouble With Weddings	*Freshman Frenzy*
California Crazy	*Mystery Letters*
Second-Best Friend	*Eight Is Enough*
Good-Bye, Dressel Hills	*It's a Girl Thing*

ABRAM'S DAUGHTERS
Adult Fiction

The Covenant • *The Betrayal* • *The Sacrifice*
The Prodigal • *The Revelation*

ANNIE'S PEOPLE
Adult Fiction

The Preacher's Daughter • *The Englisher* • *The Brethren*

THE HERITAGE OF LANCASTER COUNTY
Adult Fiction

The Shunning • *The Confession* • *The Reckoning*

OTHER ADULT FICTION

The Postcard • *The Crossroad*
The Redemption of Sarah Cain
October Song • *Sanctuary** • *The Sunroom*

www.BeverlyLewis.com

*with David Lewis